Dear Parent:

Your child's love of reading starts here!

Every child learns to read in a different way and at his or her own speed. Some go back and forth between reading levels and read favorite books again and again. Others read through each level in order. You can help your young reader improve and become more confident by encouraging his or her own interests and abilities. From books your child reads with you to the first books he or she reads alone, there are I Can Read Books for every stage of reading:

SHARED READING
Basic language, word repetition, and whimsical illustrations, ideal for sharing with your emergent reader

BEGINNING READING
Short sentences, familiar words, and simple concepts for children eager to read on their own

READING WITH HELP
Engaging stories, longer sentences, and language play for developing readers

READING ALONE
Complex plots, challenging vocabulary, and high-interest topics for the independent reader

I Can Read Books have introduced children to the joy of reading since 1957. Featuring award-winning authors and illustrators and a fabulous cast of beloved characters, I Can Read Books set the standard for beginning readers.

A lifetime of discovery begins with the magical words **"I Can Read!"**

Visit www.icanread.com for information
on enriching your child's reading experience.

Pinkalicious®
and the Merminnies

To Brenda
—V.K.

The author gratefully acknowledges
the artistic and editorial contributions of
Daniel Griffo and Jacqueline Resnick.

I Can Read® and I Can Read Book® are trademarks of HarperCollins Publishers.

Pinkalicious and the Merminnies
Copyright © 2020 by VBK, Co.
PINKALICIOUS and all related logos and characters are trademarks of Victoria Kann. Used with permission.
Based on the HarperCollins book *Pinkalicious* written by Victoria Kann and Elizabeth Kann, illustrated by Victoria Kann.

Library of Congress Control Number: 2019944391
ISBN 978-0-06-284045-5 (trade bdg.)—ISBN 978-0-06-284044-8 (pbk.)

19 20 21 22 23 SCP 10 9 8 7 6 5 4 3 2 1
❖
First Edition

Pinkalicious®
and the Merminnies

by Victoria Kann

HARPER

An Imprint of HarperCollinsPublishers

"I can't wait to meet your cousin!"

I said to my friend Aqua.

Aqua and her cousin are merminnies.

Merminnies are miniature merpeople!

"You'll love Splash!" Aqua said.

She waved at her cousin,

who was juggling three sea stars.

"Presenting Splash the Mermazing!"
Aqua said with a laugh.

"Come meet my friends!"
she called.

The waves crashed loudly.

"What did you say?" Splash asked.

"Do more tricks for your friends?"

Splash balanced on a turtle.

"Presenting—EEK!" Splash squeaked.

His tail slipped.

He splashed into the sea.

"I meant to do that!" he called.

"Now will you come ashore?"

Aqua called to Splash.

"You want an encore?" Splash asked.

"He can't hear me." Aqua groaned.

"He's too far away," Peter said.

"Then we have to be louder," I said.

"We can use conch shells as horns!"

We waved and yelled

and jumped up and down.

"A standing ovation?" Splash gasped.

"What a great audience!"

He took a bow.

"I have one more trick," Splash said.

"Meet my friend Tiny."

"Pinkawow!" I said.

Tiny wasn't tiny.

She was a huge whale!

The whale spouted water.

Splash rode on her spray!

Splash did a flip in midair.

Oh no!

Now he was too far away

from the whale's spray!

Splash was going to fall!

Splash crashed down to the sea.

"I meant to do that!" he called up.

He pulled at his tail.

It was stuck in seaweed!

"I'll go help him," Aqua said.

"I wish we could come too,"
I said, "but it's too far to swim."

Suddenly I saw a ripple in the water.

It was the turtles!

"They're making a path for you,"

said Aqua.

"So we can go help Splash!" I said.

We hopped from turtle to turtle.

"It's turtle hopscotch!" Peter said.

Finally we got to Splash.

"Meet Pinkalicious and Peter,"

Aqua said.

"Am I glad to see you," Splash said.

"I could really use a hand!"

"Or a tail!" Aqua said.

We all worked together

to untangle Splash.

Seaweed went everywhere.

Some landed on my head.

"You look like a mermaid!"

said Peter.

Seaweed stuck to Peter's head too.

"You look like you are

king of the sea!" I said.

"I'm free!" Splash gasped at last.
"Thanks to my old sea friends
and my new ones too!"
Splash was so happy
that he spun around
three times in the water.

24

Peter and I laughed.

"Splash is silly," Peter said.

"I know just how to thank you,"

said Splash.

He whispered something to Tiny.

Tiny spouted water.

"Time to take a ride!" Splash said.

"Me first!" Peter said.

Peter zoomed up into the air

on Tiny's spray!

"Your turn!" Peter told me.

I felt a little scared.

Aqua swam over.

"Do you want to ride together?"
Aqua asked.

"Yes—thank you," I said.

Whoosh!

We soared into the air.

It was mermazing!

"I'm flying!" I said.

"I can fly too!" Splash said.

He grabbed onto a seagull's tail.

The bird carried him up and up.

Splash waved hello

and lost his balance.

"Oops!" he said.

He fell into the waves.

"That was fun!" Splash said.

We all laughed.

"Splash knows how
to make a splash!" I said.